MORRIS
THE MOUSE HUNTER

Also by Vivian French

Morris and the Cat Flap
Morris in the Apple Tree
Guinea Pigs on the Go
Guinea Pigs go to Sea

More Roaring Good Reads from Collins

The Littlest Dragon *by Margaret Ryan*
Spider McDrew *by Alan Durant*
Daisy May *by Jean Ure*
Witch-in-Training: Flying Lessons *by Maeve Friel*
Mister Skip *by Michael Morpurgo*

MORRIS
THE MOUSE HUNTER

Vivian French

Illustrations by Olivia Villet

ROARING GOOD READS

Collins

An imprint of HarperCollinsPublishers

First published in Great Britain by CollinsChildren'sBooks in 1995
This edition published in Great Britain by Collins in 2003
Collins is an imprint of HarperCollins*Publishers* Ltd
77-85 Fulham Palace Road, Hammersmith, London W6 8JB

The HarperCollins website address is www.**fire**and**water**.com

1 3 5 7 9 8 6 4 2

Text copyright © Vivian French 1995
Illustrations © Olivia Villet 2003

ISBN 0 00 714732 5

Vivien French asserts the moral right to be
identified as the author of the work.
Olivia Villet asserts the moral right to be
identified as the illustrator of the work.

Printed and bound in England by Clays Ltd, St Ives plc

For Bonnie,
a cat with great charm
like her owner, Fiona

Chapter One

Morris was ginger and white, and
very fat.

"Morris," said his mother, "you're much too fat."

"That's right," said his big sister Rose.
"What you need is exercise."
"Exercise?" said Morris. "What's that?"

His mother looked at him.

"Running and jumping," she said.

"And bouncing and pouncing," said
his little brother Tom. He bounced up
and down. "Like me!"

"Oh," said Morris. He licked his paw. "I'm very good at licking and purring," he said. "And I'm EVER so good at eating."

"We know," said his mother.

"But now it's time for running and jumping."

"Must I?" said Morris.

"Yes," said his mother.

Morris began by running. He ran to his
food bowl, and he ate up every
little scrap.

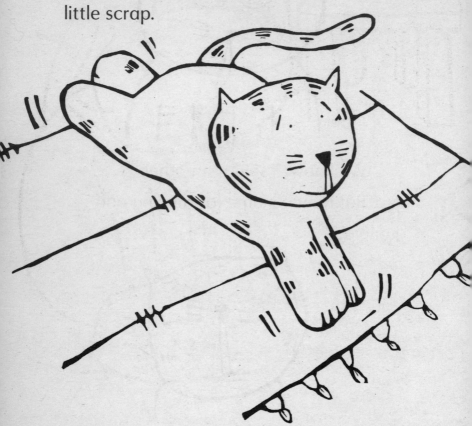

"I've done my running," he said.
"Can I have a rest?"

"No," said his mother. "You must do some jumping first."

Morris sighed. "All right," he said,
and he jumped on to the large cosy
chair in the kitchen. Then he curled up
and went to sleep.

Chapter Two

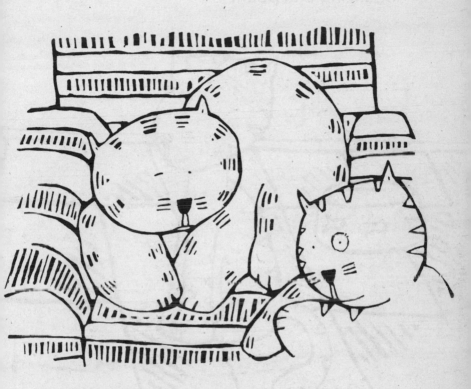

"Morris, Morris! Wake up!"

Morris woke up. Rose was pulling his tail.

"Come along," she said. "It's time for your exercise. You haven't done any bouncing and pouncing."

"Must I?" said Morris.

"Yes," said Rose.

Morris bounced up to his food bowl,
but it was empty.

"I can't bounce any more," he said.
"I'm too hungry."

His mother shook her head. "It's not
time for dinner yet," she said.

"You've got to pounce like me,"
said Tom. He pounced on Morris's
paws, and he pounced on Morris's tail.
"Like that," he said.

"Then can I have my dinner?"
Morris asked.

"We'll see," said his mother.

Morris found a fly buzzing at the window, and pounced. The fly buzzed away, and Morris sat down.

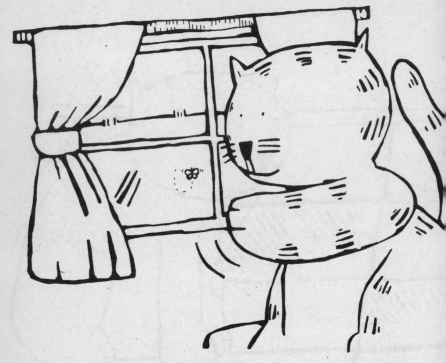

"I'm tired," he said.

"Come along," said his mother, "I want to see you pouncing."

"I've pounced," said Morris. "It buzzed off. Can I have my dinner now?"

"No," said his mother. "One run and one jump and one bounce and one pounce isn't enough." She scratched her ears. "What do you think, Rose?"

Rose stroked her whiskers.

"I know," she said. "Morris can go and catch a mouse."

Morris stared. "A MOUSE?"

"Yes," said Rose.

Morris began to cry. "You said I could have my dinner if I pounced," he sobbed, "and I did. I pounced on a fly. Why can't I have my dinner? It's not fair."

His mother jumped up on to the large cosy chair.

"You need exercise," she said.

"You go and find a mouse, and be sure to run and jump and bounce and pounce. Then you can have your dinner." And she curled up and went to sleep.

Rose began to wash Tom's ears.
"Hurry up, Morris," she said. "You'll
never catch a mouse if you sit and cry."

Chapter Three

Morris walked slowly out of the kitchen.

He went slowly up the stairs to the bedroom and into the bathroom. There was no sign of a mouse.

He came slowly down the stairs and into the sitting room, but there was no mouse there either.

"Where can I find a mouse?" he said
to himself. "Everyone is very mean. All I
want is my dinner."

"Morris!" said Rose. Morris jumped.
"Morris, are you looking for a mouse?"
Morris nodded.

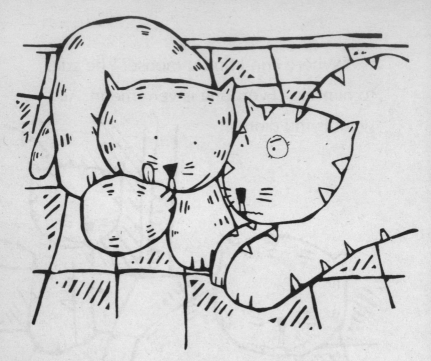

"Good," said Rose. "Mind you sit
very still."

Morris nodded again. He sat down
and licked his paw.

There was a little noise in the corner
of the room. Morris stopped licking his
paw and looked up.

"What's that?" he said.

"Ssssh!" said Rose. "You mustn't say, 'What's that?' You must crouch down and watch and listen."

"Oh," said Morris. "All right." He crouched down and watched and listened. Nothing happened.

Morris sat up again and looked at his paws.

"Bother," he said. "I can't remember which one I've licked. Perhaps I'd better start again."

There was another little noise. A little scratching noise. Morris licked his paws.

"Morris!" said Rose. "What did I tell you?"

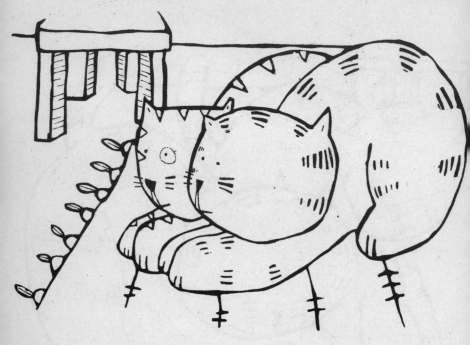

"Oh yes," said Morris, and he crouched down. The noise went on scratching. Morris went on watching and listening.

After two minutes Morris was bored.

"What do I do now?" he asked in a loud voice.

"SSSSH!" said Rose. She was crouching down beside Morris, and her eyes were gleaming.

Morris yawned.

"BE QUIET!" hissed Rose.

Morris was.

From under the book shelves in the
corner of the room crept a small grey
mouse. Morris stared at it. The mouse
crept a little closer.

"NOW!" said Rose.

"Now what?" asked Morris.

"MERRROW!" said Rose, and she sprang at the mouse. The mouse slid away under Morris's nose and out of the door. Rose sprang after it and Morris heard them rushing through the kitchen.

"Well, well," said Morris.

Chapter Four

There was another little scratching
noise. Morris looked up and saw
another mouse tiptoeing out. A small fat
mouse, with drooping whiskers. She
stopped when she saw Morris, and her
nose trembled.

"Hello," said Morris.

"Eek!" said the mouse.

Morris scratched his ears.

"Aren't you going to jump and pounce at me?" the mouse asked.

"Do you want me to?" said Morris.

"Not really," said the mouse. "But my mother says that's what cats do. She says cats run and jump and bounce and pounce, and mice run away.

That's how mice stay thin, my mother says. They run and run." The mouse sighed. "My mother says I can't have my dinner until I've done some running."

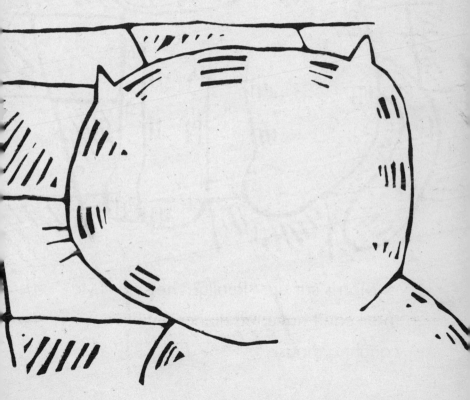

Morris sat up. "Really?" he said. "Me too. I can't have my dinner until I've caught a mouse."

The mouse and Morris looked at each other. Morris shook his head.

"I don't want to catch you," he said.
"I don't want to run and run," said the mouse.

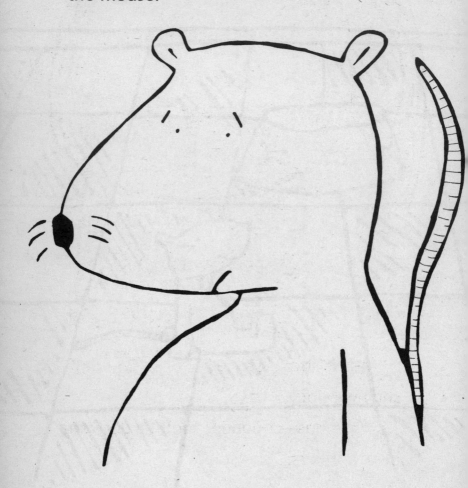

Morris stroked his whiskers. "So what shall we do?"

The mouse coughed. "You've got very nice whiskers," she said.

Morris began to purr.

"If I had a cat's whisker," the mouse said, "my mother might think I had run and run."

Morris stopped purring. "But that would hurt," he said.

"You can have one of my whiskers," the mouse said. "Then your mother might think you had run and jumped and bounced and pounced on me."

"Hurrah!" said Morris.

Morris and the mouse each pulled out a whisker.

"OW!" said the mouse.

"OW!" said Morris.

The mouse tucked Morris's whisker
under her arm. "Thank you very much,"
she said. "I hope you get your dinner
now."

"Thank YOU," said Morris. He looked at the mouse. "If ever you want to share my dinner," he said, "you'd be most welcome."

"I'll remember that," said the mouse, and she smiled.

Chapter Five

"MERRROW!" said Rose and Tom and
Morris's mother from the doorway.

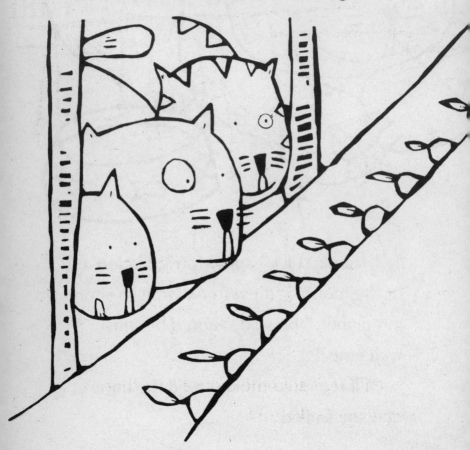

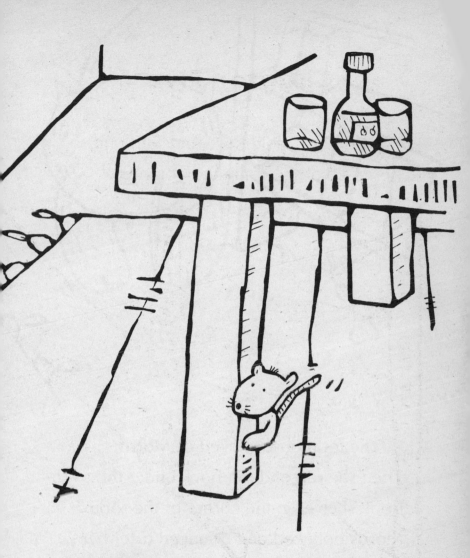

"EEEEK," said the mouse's mother
from under the table.

The fat mouse winked at Morris.
Then she ran and ran back under the
book shelves in the corner of the room.
Morris bounced and pounced after her.
Then he turned round, with the whisker
in his mouth.

"WOW!" said Tom.

"WELL DONE, MORRIS!" said Rose.

"GOOD BOY, MORRIS!" said his mother.

Morris purred. He thought he heard
the mouse's mother saying, "GOOD
GIRL!" from under the book shelves in
the corner, and he purred louder.

"I think," said Morris's mother, "that it's time for dinner!"

Morris ran and jumped and bounced and pounced all the way to his dinner bowl.

The End